D0699056

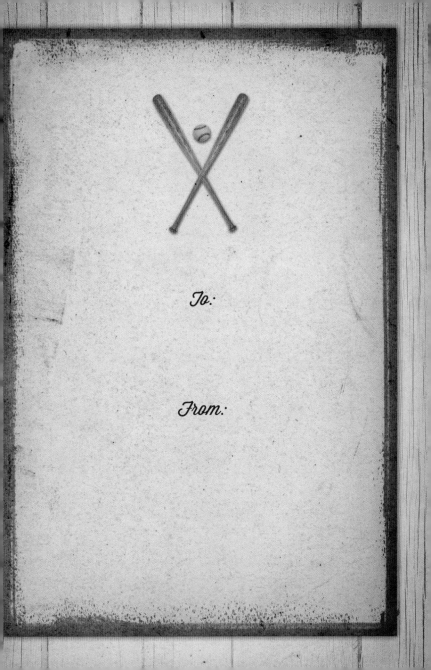

To:

From:

BASEBALL, BOYS,
and BAD WORDS

Published in Nashville, Tennessee, by Thomas Nelson. Thomas Nelson is a
registered trademark of Thomas Nelson, Inc.

Thomas Nelson, Inc., titles may be purchased in bulk for educational,
business, fund-raising, or sales promotional use. For information, please
e-mail SpecialMarkets@ThomasNelson.com.

Printed in Mexico

13 14 15 16 RRD 6 5 4 3 2

BASEBALL, BOYS, and BAD WORDS

ANDY ANDREWS

THOMAS NELSON

Since 1798

NASHVILLE   DALLAS   MEXICO CITY   RIO DE JANEIRO

BASEBALL

WAS, IS, AND ALWAYS

WILL BE TO ME THE

BEST GAME

IN THE **WORLD.**

—*Babe Ruth*

Baseball has been called the national pastime and rightly so because it stands for the fair play, clean living, and good sportsmanship which are our national heritage. That is why it has such a warm place in our hearts.

—Franklin D. Roosevelt, August 5, 1936

In a town without a movie theater or fast-food restaurant, life is divided into three distinct seasons: football, basketball, and baseball. Weeks, months, and, yes, time itself revolves around the children, their practices, and games. Most kids played all three sports, but at eleven years of age I didn't weigh enough to play football and measurements for basketball had me at a lofty four-foot-five. It was baseball for me and had been for several years. This year, however, I was going to be a "starter" at second base.

People ask me what I do in winter when there's no baseball. I'll tell you what I do. I stare out the window and wait for spring.

—Rogers Hornsby

As we milled around, one could easily pick out the kids from last year's team: Lee Peyton, Steve Krotzer, Phillip Wilson, Charles Raymond Floyd, and, of course, me. We all had on last year's hats. They were off-white with a dark-blue bill and a big "FNB" on the front.

First National Bank, our sponsor, would be giving everyone new hats. We knew that, but in the meantime we wanted to be sure that our new coach could tell the veterans from the rookies.

None of us had met our new coach. His name was Mr. Simpson. He was, we were told, "new to the area." "New to the area" and "new in town" were two different things. If someone was "new in town," that generally meant they had moved from someplace we had heard of and were probably still within driving distance of their cousins. "New to the area," however, was a hint that this person was "from the North."

Living, as we did, in the southern part of Alabama, "North" to me was Birmingham. At the time, I suppose I was somewhat suspicious of people from the North. To be certain, it was a tiny distinction, yet the phrase brought visions of Vikings and pillaging to my mind. This created an intense curiosity about Mr. Simpson—almost a feeling of danger. After all, I had been told more than once that these people could be nice, but they were different. The word *different* was always articulated with a pause and with eyebrows raised.

Mr. Simpson parked his station wagon and gathered the equipment from the back. Bats, balls, catcher's gear. Yep, it was all there. We were watching him from the backstop as if he were some wild animal at the zoo. We noticed a boy with him. The boy had red hair and more freckles than I had seen on any human since my Aunt Nancy Jane (and she had freckles on her fingernails!). The boy, we figured, was the coach's son since Mr. Simpson also had red hair and more than his share of freckles.

On June 6, 1939, the first Little League game was played in Williamsport, Pennsylvania.

"Hi, boys," Mr. Simpson said as he dumped the equipment near home plate. "My name is Hankin Simpson, and I'm your new coach."

I glanced to my right. Kevin Perkins was smirking and looking at me. Kevin was kind of a smart aleck, and I knew what he was thinking: *Hankin? Where did he come from?*

Placing his hand on the shoulder of the redheaded boy, Mr. Simpson continued, "I want you to meet my son. This is Hankin Jr."

I didn't dare look toward Kevin. I didn't need to.

I could hear him smirking from where I was.

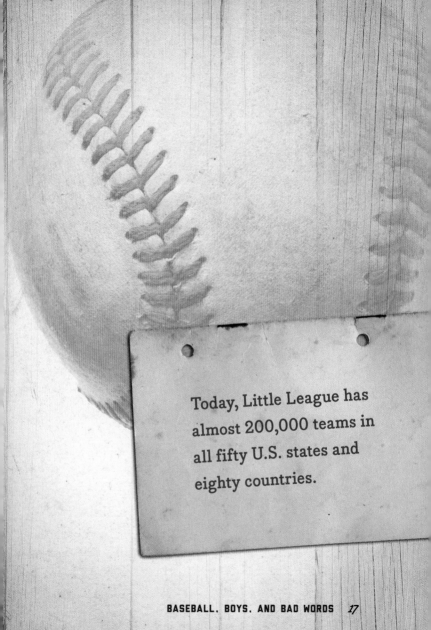

Today, Little League has almost 200,000 teams in all fifty U.S. states and eighty countries.

"Now, boys," the coach continued, "I'm new to the area."

Well, I thought, *that explains* "Hankin."

"But I'm sure," he said, "that it's going to be a great season. Okay? Okay! Now, before we begin to practice, take a rap!" And with that, he clapped his hands and busied himself arranging the equipment.

We shuffled our feet and looked at each other. *What*, we wondered, *did he want us to do? Take a what?*

A rap? What was a rap?

Little League baseball is a very good thing because it keeps the parents off the streets.

—*Yogi Berra*

Hankin Jr., we saw, had begun to trot around the field, and figuring that he knew what he was doing, we trotted after him.

"*Rap* is a Northern word," whispered Phillip as we jogged along. "It means 'to run.'"

I wasn't sure whether to believe him or not. Kevin was a smart aleck, but Phillip Wilson made things up. He was what five-year-olds called a storyteller, what we called a fibber, and what adults called a liar. He could look you right in the eye, tell you a fib, and would be so convincing that you never doubted a word he said. I kept him as a friend because I had heard my dad tell my mom that Phillip was certain to become president one day.

THERE ARE THIRTY TEAMS IN MAJOR
LEAGUE BASEBALL TODAY. THROUGHOUT
HISTORY THERE HAVE BEEN MANY MORE,
INCLUDING THE WORCESTER RUBY LEGS
AND THE NEWARK PEPPER.

Back at home plate, all out of
breath from running a rap, we gathered
around Mr. Simpson, quite sure that
he would now assign positions. We
veterans thrust our caps toward his
face, a virtual sea of FNBs, silently
pleading with the man not to look at
one of us and say, "Right field."

Since time began, all Little Leaguers have had a fear of right field. There are nine positions on a baseball diamond, and in the glamour department, right field ranks dead last.

Most batters are right-handed and hit the ball to left field; therefore, a coach who wants to avoid long losing streaks will naturally put his weakest player in "right."

Although professional baseball began during the 1800s, the first World Series of the modern era was in 1903. The Boston Americans beat the Pittsburgh Pirates five games to three.

I'd had my brush with this humiliation two years earlier as the weak link for Henley's Hardware Store (green hat, white *H*). Standing in right field game after game with nary a ball hit my way, I never believed the adults who told me I was an integral part of the team. I couldn't catch, but I wasn't stupid. A permanent residence in right field was an embarrassment. It was a curse. I was certain that I had been branded for the rest of my life. I could imagine myself as a grown-up going to a job interview and being told, "We're sorry, but there's just no place for you at NASA. We see on your record that you played right field."

There is always
some kid who may
be seeing me for the
first or last time. I
owe him my best.

—Joe DiMaggio

"Boys," Mr. Simpson began, "we're going to be winners this year. I'm excited about this team. Before we get going, I want to check you out on certain positions. Don't worry if you're new to the game. On my team everyone gets to pray."

Excuse me? Did he say "pray"? I looked at Steve Krotzer. He was jabbing Charles Raymond Floyd in the ribs. Lee Peyton was jabbing Kevin and Phillip jabbed me.

"I know this is just practice," the coach continued, "but no matter. I want you to pray your hearts out!"

This team, I thought, *is in trouble*. Either someone had told our new leader that last year we lost seventeen out of twenty-three games, or he took one look at us and decided that we were a bunch of rejects. What it boiled down to, I was beginning to believe, was that if we were to have any chance of a winning season, Mr. Simpson had settled on prayer as our only hope.

Thirty minutes later we were in the positions that would be ours, more or less, for the rest of the season. I was at second base, so I was happy. Steve was at first, Kevin at third, Lee was our catcher, and Charles Raymond stood in right field with the other kids who couldn't catch.

There is no room in baseball for discrimination. It is our national pastime and a game for all.

—*Lou Gehrig*

Phillip Wilson, meanwhile, pouted at shortstop. He wanted to pitch. Actually, we wanted him to pitch too, but as soon as we had seen that there was a Hankin Simpson Jr., we knew that he would not. Every member of First National Bank was acutely aware of that age-old Little League law: if the coach has a son, the team has a pitcher.

This has become such an accepted part of coaching methodology that it is no longer questioned. A Little League coach is usually the father of one of the players, and he always has a blind spot where his child is concerned. Can the kid throw strikes? Has he got a curveball? Does he trip over his own feet? None of that really matters; he's the coach's son. Put him on the mound. He's a pitcher.

We practiced hard that first day. Trying to show Mr. Simpson our "stuff," we dove for grounders, swung for the fence, and generally showed as much hustle as we could muster. We didn't seem to be a vastly improved team from the year before. I blew a sure double play, our new pitcher was throwing the ball over the backstop, and Charles Raymond got hit in the head by a pop fly and cried.

I want to be remembered as a ballplayer who gave all I had to give.

—Roberto Clemente

Coach Simpson didn't say much, but when he did, he was still saying things we didn't understand: "Take another rap. Pray hard, pray hard!" We were a confused group of kids. It was at the end of practice, however, during the compulsory pep talk, when everything became crystal clear.

"There is one thing about this game you can count on," he said. "If you don't rearn to watch the basebarr hit the basebarr grove, you wirr never be an excerrent basebarr prayer."

I think about baseball when I wake up in the morning. I think about it all day and I dream about it at night. The only time I don't think about it is when I'm playing it.

—Carl Yastrzemski

Well, we were stunned. After two and a half hours of total darkness, we suddenly understood. A rap? Pray? He had wanted us to take a *lap*! He had wanted us to *play* hard! How could we have been so blind?

From the depths of a pep talk to which no one was listening—like a bolt from the blue—those weird words all came together and made sense. Certain words from his last sentence jumped out at us like sparks from a bonfire. "Blah, blah, blah, *rearn,* blah, blah, blah, *basebarr,* blah, blah, *basebarr grove*, blah, blah, *wirr*, blah, blah, blah, *excerrent basebarr prayer.*"

It was now an undeniable fact that had become apparent to us all in one fell swoop. Coach Simpson could not say his *L*s!

We stood silently exchanging furtive glances, as Hankin Jr. and Sr. got in their car and drove away. No one had spoken a word yet, but we suspected that we had been the recipients of a miracle from God. We could scarcely contain our collective excitement. To a group of eleven-year-old boys, nothing beats having a human target at which to laugh. Double the fun if the boys are able to mimic the target, and triple if the unfortunate target happens to be an adult!

I ain't ever had a job. I just always played baseball.

—Satchel Paige

Kevin was smirking again. We shuffled around and snickered a bit. Then it started.

Charles Raymond: **"I'm a basebarr prayer."**

Steve: **"No, you ain't. You're a right fierder!"**

Kevin: **"Take a rap! Take a rap!"**

Phillip: **"Did you hear him call me Phirrip?"**

Lee: **"Coach Simpson? I rike him. I rearry do!"**

And so it continued until we were exhausted. Finally, able to breathe at last, we lounged in the dirt around home plate. Phillip spoke first, this time seriously. "I think he's Oriental," he said. "Oriental people use the letter *R* in place of the letter *L* when they speak English because they don't have the letter *L* in their own language. That's why he does it. Coach Simpson is Oriental. Remember? He said he was new to the area . . . he's Oriental."

"Oriental?" Charles Raymond asked. "Isn't that when you know your way around?"

Kevin smirked. "No, Stupe," he said. "He means Japanese, right?"

Kevin glanced my way. I wanted to tell Phillip that I had never seen a six-foot-three-inch, 240-pound, redheaded, freckle-faced Japanese guy before. That's what I wanted to say, but Phillip was looking at me with such an air of self-confidence that I knew the truth did not stand a chance against such a convincing opponent.

I was about to give it a try anyway when Lee suddenly giggled.

"What?" we demanded.

"I was just thinking . . . ," Lee said as he tried to talk through his laughter. "I was just thinking that this year sometime, I'm gonna be rounding third . . ."

He stopped and laughed. "I'm gonna be rounding third headed toward this here home plate and . . ." He was really laughing now.

"Tell us," we urged.

"I'm gonna be headed toward this here home plate, and Coach Simpson's gonna yell, 'Sride, Ree! Sride!'"

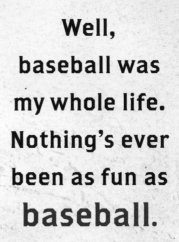

Well, baseball was my whole life. Nothing's ever been as fun as **baseball.**

—*Mickey Mantle*

We never mentioned the Oriental theory again. Kevin told me privately one day that he thought Phillip was "full of mess." I took that to be Kevin's way of saying that he didn't believe Coach Simpson was Japanese either. Not that it would have mattered. One of our best friends, Peter Chin, was Japanese. He said his *L*s perfectly, except, of course, when he was mimicking Coach Simpson with us.

Several memories of that year still remain clear in my mind. To this day, Phillip Wilson is "Phirrip" to everyone who played on that team. And no one has forgotten the game that Lee Peyton rounded third, headed for home, and fell down laughing before he got there, because Coach Simpson really did yell,

"Sride,
Ree!
Sride!"

If I had to choose one capsule of time during that season to carry with me for the rest of my life, it would have to be the day Steve Krotzer got kicked off the team. Maybe *kicked off* is too harsh. Actually, he was transferred to another team because the league president found that Steve's family was living in another district.

There are
only two
seasons:
WINTER
and
BASEBALL.

—Bill Veeck

It was a messy situation. Steve had played with us for four years. Two years on Henley's Hardware Store and two with First National Bank. Now they were sending him to play with the team—Sand Dollar Shoes—near his home. We were sick about it. Steve was our friend and a darn good first baseman. He didn't want to go. We didn't want him to leave. But that last day did arrive.

When practice was over, Coach Simpson gathered us around the pitcher's mound. He had his hand on Steve's shoulder. "Boys," he said, "this is a sad day. We're going to miss Steve. He's a fine barr prayer and a fine young man."

Steve was close to tears.

We were too.

"I don't understand the inner workings of the system," Coach Simpson continued. "And I'm not sure why this has happened. But I do know one thing . . . and rook at me when I say this because it is important. I want every one of you to know that this was not Steve's faurt."

As a group, Steve included, we jumped as if ten thousand volts of electricity had passed through our bodies. Did he say what we thought he said? Surely not.

"No," he continued. "This was not Steve's faurt, and it wasn't my faurt."

Yes, he did most definitely, absolutely say what we thought he said! Oh sure, we knew what he meant; we'd been unconsciously translating Simpsonisms all year. He was telling us that it wasn't Steve's *fault* . . . but that wasn't what we were hearing!

"It wasn't Steve's parents' faurt either. I guess it was nobody's faurt," he said.

It was too good to be true. Of all the words in the world guaranteed to make eleven-year-old boys laugh, only one of them is all by itself at the top of the list. And our coach—an adult—was saying that word over and over.

"If it's anyone's faurt, it's the system's faurt. So don't pin the faurt on any one person, because it is just not their faurt!"

Well, I am not exaggerating when I say that we were literally lying on the ground. We were crying. Coach Simpson thought we really were crying and became concerned. He sounded desperate as he tried to comfort us, but the more he explained that it wasn't our "faurt," the more out of hand things became.

Soon tears were rolling down Coach Simpson's face too. Several of us felt bad about that later, but, as Kevin pointed out, "Hey, don't worry about it. It ain't our faurt!"

I haven't seen Coach Simpson in years. Kevin Perkins and Steve Krotzer were in my wedding. Lee Peyton went to medical school and returned to practice in our town. Charles Raymond Floyd was a late bloomer. He was a center fielder in college, made second-team All American, and played three years of minor league ball. I've totally lost track of Phillip Wilson. The last I heard, he was a used car salesman and perpetually campaigning for mayor in a small town in Louisiana. Kevin, incidentally, is still my best friend, though he continues to live in our little town and I have long since moved away.

I still remember us all as we were that summer. I can close my eyes and hear the explosions of laughter as we react to something that was, to us, the funniest thing in the world.

And I feel a little sad when I think that when we were eleven years old, we may have laughed harder than we ever would again.

_____
Team Name

_____   _____   _____
Season   Wins   Losses

_____   _____
Coach   Assistant

_____   _____
Pitcher   Catcher

_____   _____
First Base   Second Base

_____   _____
Third Base   Short Stop

_____   _____
Left Field   Center Field

_____   _____
Right Field   Designated Hitter

_____   _____
Utility Player   Utility Player

_____   _____
Utility Player   Utility Player

CONTACT ANDY

To interact with Andy through Facebook and Twitter, and
learn more about his other books visit

ANDYANDREWS.COM

To book Andy for a speaking engagement, call
(800) 726-ANDY (2639)

READY TO LAUGH EVEN MORE?

In *Return to Sawyerton Springs,* the baseball story is merely
the first chapter! You'll find the same heartwarming
humor as you read story after story of a simple town
during a simpler time. *Return to Sawyerton Springs* will
engage your mind and heart while inspiring tears
of laughter as you become introduced to a cast of
unforgettable characters you'll feel like you've known
your whole life, including:

- A scheming cousin who causes more trouble than he's worth
- Two former best friends divided over a fight involving a 10-pound bass
- 17 townspeople who turn an unorthodox high school fundraiser into a memory the community will never forget

So take a deep breath, and prepare to rekindle your spirit
as you **Return to Sawyerton Springs**.

ISBN: 978-0-9819709-1-2

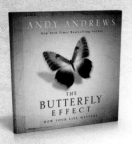

THE
BUTTERFLY
EFFECT

HOW YOUR LIFE MATTERS

ISBN: 978-1-4041-8780-1

"Every single thing you do matters. You have been created as one of a kind. You have been created in order to make a difference. You have within you the power to change the world."

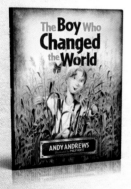

The **Boy** Who
Changed the **World**

Everything You Do Matters

ISBN: 978-1-4003-1605-2

The Boy Who Changed the World reveals the incredible truth that everything YOU do matters—what you did yesterday, what you do today, and what you will do tomorrow. Every choice you make, good or bad, can make a difference.